FIX-IT

by David McPhail

E. P. Dutton   New York

for Ann, who helped

Unicorn is a registered trademark of E. P. Dutton.
Library of Congress number 83-16459
ISBN 0-525-44323-1
Published in the United States by E. P. Dutton,
2 Park Avenue, New York, N.Y. 10016,
a division of NAL Penguin Inc.
Published simultaneously in Canada by
Fitzhenry & Whiteside Limited, Toronto
Editor: Ann Durell   Designer: Isabel Warren-Lynch
Printed in Hong Kong by South China Printing Co.
First Unicorn Edition 1987   COBE
10 9 8 7 6 5 4 3 2

One morning Emma got up early
to watch television.

But the TV didn't work.

Emma asked her mother to fix it.

"Hurry, Mom!" she cried.

Emma's mother tried to fix it.

But she couldn't.

Emma's father tried.

But he couldn't fix it, either.

So he called the fix-it man. "Please hurry," he said. "It's an emergency!"

The fix-it man came right away.

He tried to fix the TV. Emma's mother
and father tried to fix Emma.

Her father blew up a balloon...

until it popped.

Her mother sang a song.

So did the cat.

Her father pretended to be a horse—
but Emma didn't feel like riding.

Finally her mother read her a book.

"Read it again," said Emma when her
mother had finished.

"And again."

"And again."

"Now *I'll* read to Millie," said Emma.
And she went to her room.

Then her father found out what was
wrong with the TV.

"I fixed it!" he called.

But Emma didn't come out of her room.

She was too busy.